W9-AGQ-440

Weekly Reader Children's Book Club presents

THE TREASURE OF
TOPO-EL-BAMPO

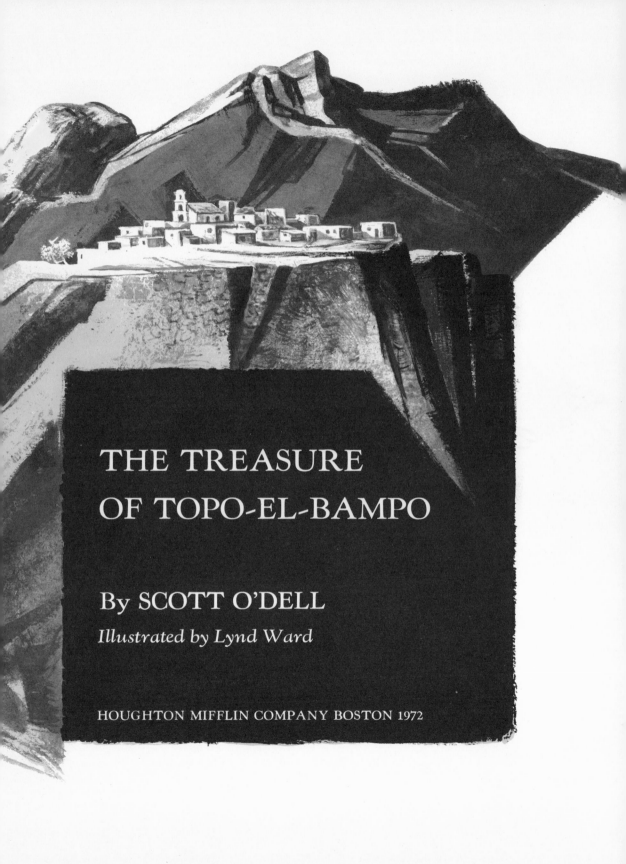

THE TREASURE
OF TOPO-EL-BAMPO

By SCOTT O'DELL

Illustrated by Lynd Ward

HOUGHTON MIFFLIN COMPANY BOSTON 1972

Books by
SCOTT O'DELL

The Black Pearl
The Dark Canoe
Island of the Blue Dolphins
Journey to Jericho
The King's Fifth
Sing Down the Moon

WEEKLY READER
CHILDREN'S BOOK CLUB
This is a registered trademark

COPYRIGHT © 1972 BY SCOTT O'DELL
COPYRIGHT © 1972 BY LYND WARD
ALL RIGHTS RESERVED. NO PART OF THIS WORK MAY BE
REPRODUCED OR TRANSMITTED IN ANY FORM BY ANY MEANS,
ELECTRONIC OR MECHANICAL, INCLUDING PHOTOCOPYING AND
RECORDING, OR BY ANY INFORMATION STORAGE OR RETRIEVAL
SYSTEM, WITHOUT PERMISSION IN WRITING FROM THE PUBLISHER.
LIBRARY OF CONGRESS CATALOG CARD NUMBER 72-135138
ISBN 0-395-12576-6 ISBN 0-395-12577-4 DOL.
PRINTED IN THE U.S.A.
WEEKLY READER CHILDREN'S BOOK CLUB EDITION

To Lauren Di Prima

Long ago, two hundred years ago almost, the poorest village in
all Mexico was Topo-el-Bampo. Not one person in the village was
rich. Not the grocer nor the baker nor the man who sold sandals
and straw hats, candles, charcoal and cooking pots. Not even the
mayor, Francisco Flores, was rich.

As a matter of fact, the mayor was one of the poorest in Topo-el-Bampo. This was because he had to buy food for a wife and nine children and Grandmother Serafina, who was one hundred years old and toothless but still ate a lot.

And besides his wife and grandmother and the nine children he had two donkeys. The donkeys were small yet they had big appetites. Tiger, the smaller of the two, could eat a handful of corn at a gulp. Leandro, the other donkey, took his time and munched slowly, but he always ate more than Tiger.

The two little burros ate so much that the mayor didn't know what to do with them. He would walk up and down the house, pulling on his beard. Then he would stop and say in a loud voice, so that his wife and Grandmother Serafina and his nine children could hear, "These animals are eating us out of house and home. They eat more than all twelve of us put together. One of these days I'll sell them both."

When he spoke like this, as he often did, the children listened, for he was not only their father but also the mayor of Topo-el-Bampo. But they really didn't believe that he would ever sell the two burros. Tiger and Leandro were like members of the family. They even came into the house and walked around and begged for food.

Tiger was small for a burro. He was bigger than a jack rabbit but not by much. You could hit him with a stick and he never got angry. Nor did he get angry when Leandro gave him a nip or two. He was called Tiger only as a joke. At heart he was as mild as a mouse. He was also the color of a mouse.

Leandro, on the other hand, was twice the size of Tiger. He had long white teeth and a glossy coat that looked like chocolate pudding.

Pulling hard on his black beard, Francisco said one morning at breakfast, "I have made up my mind. I am going to sell these two animals. The first man who comes along with ten silver *duros* can have them. And I'll throw in the wooden saddles to boot."

The small house became quiet. This was the first time that Francisco had ever spoken so firmly. Seven of the children—Juan and Juanita, the twins, Tomás and Arturo, Delfina, Ysabel and Elena—began to sniffle. Rosa and Ramón, who were the oldest, only bit their lips.

María, their mother, said, "How can you be so cruel? It is like selling two of our own children. Why don't you set Tiger and Leandro loose and let them graze on the mountain?"

"Graze on the mountain?" The mayor snorted. "Graze on what? On the stones? On the thorns? And what do the burros drink on the mountain? There is no water on the mountain. There is little water here in the village. And the corn bins are nearly empty."

What the mayor said was true.

Topo-el-Bampo sat high on a rocky ridge. Around it were wild canyons covered with thorn trees and cactus. There were no streams or wells. When it rained, those who lived in the village gathered the water in ditches and stored it under the ground. They planted corn and carried water to it in jars. After the corn grew ripe they stored it away in bins and lived on it during the long, dry winters. Sometimes after winter was over, no corn was left in the bins and everyone went hungry.

That was what happened one year, at the end of a bad winter, before a new crop of corn could be planted and harvested. The people of Topo-el-Bampo went hungry. The mayor and his family went hungry. The village priest, Father Bruno, went hungry. All the burros and goats went hungry. Everyone lived on roots they

dug on the mountainside. And the animals ate what the people left.

That was why the mayor at last carried out his threat. Why he sold his two burros to the first man who came along, the man from the Mine of the Three Brothers.

At the foot of the mountain, right below the village of Topo-el-Bampo, sat the Mine of the Three Brothers. It was the finest silver mine in Mexico. As a matter of fact, it was the finest silver mine in the world. Silver poured out of the mine day after day, even at night.

This silver was melted into bars and the bars were strapped on the backs of burros who carried it down to the harbor of Mazatlán. From there it went by ship around Cape Horn and across the ocean to the King of Spain.

Because this great treasure poured out of the mine day and night, it took many burros, hundreds of them, to carry the silver bars from the mine to Mazatlán. The trip was long and hard and dangerous. The burros soon wore out. And that was why every year men had to go into the mountains and through the countryside in search of more burros.

The man from the Mine of the Three Brothers came early in
the morning as the sun was just rising over the thorn-tree forest.
The two burros were in the small corral next to the house. The
man looked at them and grunted.

"They're too skinny to carry a load of silver," he said to Francisco.

"They'll fatten up," Francisco said.

The man from the mine took a leather bag from his coat and
counted out seven coins. "They're not worth seven," he said.

Francisco, the mayor, shook his head. "Ten," he said.

The children stood in a line beside the corral and prayed. They
prayed that their father would not take the seven *duros*. That the
man from the mine would not pay ten. That Tiger and Leandro,
therefore, would not be sold.

"Eight *duros*," the man from the mine said.

"Ten," Francisco said.

The man paused. "Nine *duros*," he said. "That is my last offer."

He started to put the coins back in his leather bag. The children watched their father. They held their breath and waited.

"Nine," the man said.

Francisco held out his hand and took the nine silver *duros*, which were worth nine dollars. Then he went into the house and shut the door. The man from the mine tossed a rope around the neck of each of the burros and rode off. The children knew that the silver *duros* would buy many pounds of pink beans and many sacks of flour. They knew that they would not be hungry any longer, but they were very unhappy.

Silently they watched the two little burros trot down the street behind the man and his horse. They watched them start down the mountain trail. As Tiger and Leandro disappeared among the trees, all the children, except Rosa and Ramón, began to cry.

For a moment Ramón looked as if he wanted to cry, too. Then he said, "Father will buy another pair of burros one of these days."

"Yes," said Rosa, "very soon."

At this good news, the children quit crying.

But then Ramón spoiled it all. "They'll be better than Leandro and Tiger," he said. "Much better. You'll see."

The thought that any burros in the world could be better than Tiger and Leandro was too much for the children. They broke out in a loud wail, which brought Father Bruno out of his hut. He came running down the village street, his brown robe flapping around his heels.

"The burros," Father Bruno said to the children, "will have all they want to eat. Much more than they had to eat here. For this you should be happy. You should smile, not cry, at their good fortune. So begin now."

The children dried their tears on their sleeves and tried to smile.

"More," Father Bruno said. "Wider. Show your pretty teeth. That's it. Now we really smile." Father Bruno waved both his arms as if he were leading a band.

"Now we sing the song of our village," he said. "Begin. Together. Louder, please. That's good. Leandro and Tiger will hear the song as they go down the trail. They will hear and think that you wish them happiness."

It is not known if Tiger and Leandro heard the happy song the children sang. It is known that at the Mine of the Three Brothers they had all the straw and corn they could eat.

They ate and ate but they also worked. They worked much harder than they did at Topo-el-Bampo. And every day. No sooner had the treasure train carried a load of silver from the mine to the harbor of Mazatlán than another load was waiting. During spring and summer they made three trips with the train. Altogether the burros traveled more than five hundred miles.

By the end of the summer their backs were sore and their bones began to show. It was then that Manuel Mota, the trainmaster, wondered if Tiger and Leandro were good for one more trip to the harbor of Mazatlán. He walked around them as they stood in the corral. He counted their bones and looked at their sore backs.

"Sebastián," he said to his helper, "what do you think of this pair?"

"Not much," said Sebastián, "but I think they can make another trip."

"To Mazatlán and back?"

"No, just to Mazatlán," said the helper.

Which meant that once Tiger and Leandro reached the harbor and the silver bars were taken from their backs they would be pushed over the cliff into the sea. This was easier than shooting them. Pushing them over the cliff also saved bullets.

The trainmaster cracked his long rawhide whip. The King's treasure was ready to go. Strapped to the backs of a long line of burros was a fortune in glittering silver bars. Each bar, shaped like a loaf of bread, was stamped with the crest of His Majesty, the King of Spain.

In the train were one hundred and twenty burros. Each one carried two silver bars. Except Leandro, who because he was the biggest carried three bars. And Tiger, who because he was the smallest carried only one.

The trainmaster glanced down the line of burros. Again he swung the long rawhide whip around his head. "*Vámonos,*" he shouted. "Let us go!"

Tiger and Leandro moved out as briskly as they could. The bells around their necks clanked. Their hoofs struck stone. The train wound down from the Mine of the Three Brothers, down the steep ravine toward the town of Dos Ríos, three miles away.

Every time the treasure train left for the harbor of Mazatlán there was a big fiesta in Dos Ríos. The three Vargas brothers closed the mine on that day and invited all the miners to come to the plaza and celebrate.

The brothers set up great tubs of red punch and carts filled with steaming tortillas. At night they sent rockets streaking into the sky and a band played merry tunes until dawn. All the miners came with their families and had a good time.

They seemed to forget that they never were paid for their work. That they were really slaves. That the Vargas Brothers gave them no money, nothing except a hut to live in and a pot of beans each day. They forgot that the mine was a thousand feet deep and had five hundred steps. And that twice every day they had to climb that ladder, hand over hand, with a heavy basket of silver ore strapped to their backs.

On this bright September morning, as the silver train wound down from the ravine, miners and their families crowded the plaza of Dos Ríos. They had been there since dawn, eating tortillas, drinking the red punch, and waiting for the first glimpse of the silver train.

A small cloud of dust rose from the ravine. The clanking of bells came on the wind, the cries of the trainmaster, the clatter of the ten men on horseback who guarded the silver treasure. The band struck up a lively tune. At this signal, the train burst forth from the ravine, and swept down the wide street that led into the plaza.

Miners and their families cheered. They cheered the three Vargas brothers, the tubs of red punch, the cartloads of tortillas, and the treasure gleaming in the sun. They cheered the burros, calling them by name as the animals passed by. Tiger they cheered most of all because he was the smallest burro in the train. Children loved him especially. One little girl loved him so much that she ran out and put a garland of flowers around his neck.

Tiger was very fond of flowers. He liked them better than hay. Now, as he trotted along at the end of the train, he didn't hear the cheers of the crowd. His mind was fixed on the string of flowers around his neck. He stretched this way and that, but he couldn't quite reach them with his teeth.

The trainmaster cracked his long rawhide whip. The train came to a halt in front of the three houses that belonged to the Vargas brothers. The houses sat side by side. They had walls more than five feet thick, courtyards filled with flowers, the sound of fountains, and the whispering footsteps of three dozen servants.

The three brothers came out and stood together, looking down at the silver train. They stroked their long, pointed beards and looked pleased.

Tiger did not see them. He was still thinking of the flowers. He rubbed against a nearby post and was about to catch hold of the garland when Leandro sidled up.

Leandro glanced right and left, looking for the trainmaster. Then, sure that he was not being watched, with a quick snap of his

long teeth he cut the garland of flowers swiftly in two, caught up one end and walked away, munching.

There was not a burro in the train who wouldn't have followed Leandro, big as he was, and tried to get the flowers back. Not one, except Tiger. There wasn't a burro, except Tiger, who wouldn't have complained in some way at such bad treatment—a small bray at least.

But Tiger made no sound. He did not move. He twisted his left ear which was lopped at the end, blinked his eyes, jerked his tail, and stood where he had been standing, beside the big iron gate.

The gate opened. Leandro strode up the stone ramp into the Vargas courtyard and Tiger and the rest of the train followed after.

"*Andale*," the trainmaster shouted at Tiger. "Move yourself."

Tiger gathered his thoughts and jumped in the nick of time as the iron gate was about to clang shut on his tail. Two months ago in June it had clanged shut on his tail, which was the reason his tail was three inches shorter than it had been when he lived in Topo-el-Bampo.

Servants came running and lifted the silver from the saddles and stacked it in the middle of the courtyard. They took off the wooden saddles and led the burros one by one to the fountain and let them drink their fill. Then they brought bags of grain and all the burros enjoyed it.

The evening before the train set off for Mazatlán was the best part of the journey. It is possible that Tiger missed the garland of wild flowers Leandro had stolen from him, but there was no way of knowing. He finished his bag of feed, lay down on the straw bed and fell asleep, though the band played in the plaza and red rockets burst in the sky.

At dawn, when the fiesta was over and the miners were on their way to the mine, the silver train was ready to leave. The three brothers came and stood side by side in the courtyard. They stroked their pointed beards and counted the silver bars on the backs of the burros and added figures in their heads.

The Vargas brothers looked at each other and smiled. It was the richest silver train ever to leave the mine. They sent for Father Soto, who went through the courtyard and blessed the burros, placing his hand on each of their heads, or trying to.

The big iron gate swung open, the trainmaster cracked his whip, and the line filed out into the street. The trainmaster and his soldiers rode off on their horses. The train fell into step behind them.

The three brothers stood on the porch and watched until the train disappeared and the last sound of the bells faded away. Then they went to the church and got down on their knees and prayed.

They prayed that God would guide the treasure train safely through the wild country and across the many rivers. And protect it from those evil men who would steal it. They prayed that the ships would weather all storms, that the silver would safely reach the King, and that he would use it wisely in the holy service of God.

And, yes, that he would not forget to pay all the money he owed them.

As the brothers prayed, the train came on the second day to the Río Mitla and because of the rains that summer found it flooded. They took three days to make the river crossing, but made it at last without the loss of a single silver bar. Leandro swam with his head held high. And Tiger bobbed across like a cork. The rest of the burros crossed, too.

On the third morning the train came to a place where two trails met the King's Road. One trail forked to the right and went to the town of Cocorit. The other trail forked to the left and climbed the mountain to the village of Topo-el-Bampo.

Tiger had made the journey from the mine to the harbor of Mazatlán three times that summer. And not once had he passed the trail to Topo-el-Bampo without turning into it.

On this morning, it was the same. No sooner had he reached the place where the trails met than he left the train and began the steep climb toward Topo-el-Bampo. He went along slowly, cropping the grass, heedless of the silver train winding on below him.

Always before, within a minute or two, an *arriero* found that Tiger had strayed and brought him back with a belt over the ears. But on this morning Tiger wasn't missed for ten minutes. In that time he had an odd encounter.

Father Bruno came riding down the trail from Topo-el-Bampo. He was moving at a good clip on his big white mule, with his robes tucked up to his knees. He was on his way to buy salt in Cocorit and in a hurry to get home before nightfall.

He saw Tiger browsing along the trail below him. From the brand on his flank and the bar of silver tied to the saddle, he knew that the burro came from the Mine of the Three Brothers. He slackened his pace.

Burros usually look much alike. But after one sharp glance Father Bruno knew. Though the animal's bones showed through his skin, though the last time they had met the little burro had had a full tail, he knew it was Tiger.

"Hola, burrito," Father Bruno called out.

He spoke in his softest voice, the one he used for burros and children. But he was a big man, deep in the chest, and his words came out strong.

Tiger went on eating, as if nothing were happening.

Father Bruno looked hard at the bar of silver tied to the saddle. It was of the purest quality. It would buy many sacks of food for the hungry people of Topo-el-Bampo, beans for a month, tortillas for two months.

Once before he had seen the treasure train moving down to Mazatlán. Burro after burro—a hundred of them and more—laden with silver had passed him as he stood beside the King's Road. The sight made his eyes pop. It made his head dizzy.

"And where does the treasure go?" the young padre asked out

34

loud. "It goes across the seas," he answered himself, "into the chests of the King of Spain to be used for war."

In his months at Topo-el-Bampo, he had put an end to men being dragged off to slave in the Mine of the Three Brothers. But he thought of the men who had been dragged away before he came.

"Surely," he said to himself, "the Mine of the Three Brothers and the King owe us one bar. One bar, at least."

He slipped down from the saddle and walked over to the burro and put a firm hand on the silver, on the thongs that bound it to the wooden saddle. Then he drew back. He turned around and walked slowly to his mule and got into the saddle.

"The silver does not belong to me," Father Bruno said. "It belongs to the village of Topo-el-Bampo. The mine has killed many of our people. But the silver does not belong to me."

He glanced over his shoulder at Tiger and the bar of silver that was as big as a loaf of bread. As he did so, Father Bruno saw below him a man on horseback searching through the brush.

"*Hola,*" he shouted down to the man. "Your burro is here."

With these words Father Bruno rode on toward Cocorit. Tiger snatched a last mouthful of grass before the man on horseback herded him onward to the waiting train.

The train moved down the trail. On the fourth day, still far from Mazatlán, came the first talk of bandits. This was the greatest of all the dangers that beset a treasure train. Only last winter the train was attacked by a bandit called Juan Q and all the silver carried off. Juan Q had been captured and thrown into jail. But there were other bands of robbers still lurking about.

At noon on the same day, a farmer left his corn patch and hailed the trainmaster.

"My cousin tells me," he said, "that Juan Q and his bandits are camped near the Río Matos."

The trainmaster raised his hand in reply but did not halt. As they drew closer to the sea, there would be a dozen such tales every day. If he stopped to check each tale the train would never reach Mazatlán. There was only one bandit in all of Mexico whom he feared. And it was impossible for him to be camped on the Río Matos. Juan Q was in jail, safely behind prison bars.

But this time the trainmaster should have listened to what the farmer told him. On this day the trainmaster made a big mistake. Juan Q was not in jail. At that very moment he and his men were camped nearby, as the farmer had said. Juan Q had been out of prison for more than two days, waiting with his men at the Río Matos.

In the past Juan Q had attacked the silver train several times. In two of the attacks he had lost more than half his men and captured no treasure. In the last attack he had lost nobody and captured more than twenty bars of silver. It had cost him four bars to buy his way out of prison, but still he had made a good profit.

Sitting on a log with his men, Juan Q kept his eyes fixed on the King's Road as it wound down from the hills. The silver train would not reach the river for an hour. There was time for a small siesta, but he fought back the urge to sleep. With the train carrying the largest hoard of silver ever to leave the Mine of the Three Brothers, it was not the time for him to close his eyes. It was not the time to close even one eye.

The sun was overhead as the train reached the Río Matos. The trainmaster watered the burros and rested them for an hour and then sent them into the river.

From a willow grove close by, Juan Q counted the first fifty burros to trot down the bank. He watched them set out toward the far shore. He waited until ten more burros followed them. Patiently he waited until the trainmaster and his guards rode into the river, until they reached the far bank.

Now the treasure train was divided. Half was on one side of the Río Matos and half was on the other. Swiftly Juan Q rode out with his men.

At the moment Juan Q attacked the train, Leandro was halfway across the river. He had never seen Juan Q before. He had never seen any bandit before. Yet something told him that he should go no farther. Indeed, that he should turn around and go back. Go back fast, in the direction he came from. Which he did.

At the rear of the train, not having started across the river, Tiger was eating grass when Señor Q and his bandits rode out from their hiding place. He had never seen a bandit before. But he smelled trouble in the air. Quickly he slipped into the nearest thicket and waited. He stayed there motionless until all was quiet. Then he left the thicket and started back across the King's Road.

He had not gone far when Leandro came up behind him. Together the two burros took the trail that led to the town of Dos Ríos and the Mine of the Three Brothers.

On the second day of their travels, they came to the place where the King's Road forked. Here, as he always did, Tiger took the trail that climbed the mountain to Topo-el-Bampo. Leandro followed him. Cropping the summer weeds as they went, they traveled slowly, since the bars of silver they carried were heavy.

The next morning, about an hour after the sun came up, Father Bruno was seated at breakfast. It was not much of a breakfast for a strong young man, just a small bowl of wild berries and a corn cake half the size of his hand.

Father Bruno's hut was the first in the village as you came up the mountain trail. The morning was warm and he was sitting in the doorway, eating the wild berries one by one, so as to make them last longer.

He had eaten the last berry in the bowl when he heard the sound of bells. Two bells sounding out of tune, yet sweet in the hush of the morning hour.

The sound of bells grew louder and suddenly from around the last bend in the trail came two burros. They walked very slowly, barely putting one foot in front of the other, their heads bent low.

Father Bruno jumped to his feet and ran over to the big bell, which hung from a branch beside his hut. It was the one he rang to call the people of Topo-el-Bampo to church and to give alarms. He rang the bell as he had never rung it before. The sound rolled through the village. It echoed through the thorn forest. Everyone came running.

Francisco, the mayor, and his nine children came first, because they lived next door to Father Bruno. None of the nine children spoke, not Rosa nor Ramón, not Tomás nor Arturo, not Delfina, Ysabel nor Elena. They just gathered in a ring around Tiger and Leandro, patting them, feeling the burros' ears and tails, as if they couldn't believe what they saw.

Francisco shouted, "Step back. Give them air. They have come
a long way and are very tired."

"Yes," said Father Bruno, "they are very tired."

He broke his corn cake in two and gave one piece to each of
the burros.

Francisco looked at Father Bruno. They looked at each other.
They both looked at the three bars of silver on Leandro's back
and the bar on Tiger's back. Then they looked at each other again
and smiled.

Francisco untied the silver bars and handed them one by one

to Father Bruno, who carried them into his hut.

When the last heavy bar had been carried away and the saddles taken off, the little burros lay down and rolled in the dust. And all the children danced around them, singing and shouting. All except Tomás and Arturo, the youngest boys, who got down in the dust and rolled with the burros, they were so full of joy.

Francisco said, "The silver will buy many sacks of flour."

Father Bruno said, "And pink beans. Enough to last through many winters."

eNAME

J roach

yeA

Roach

It's not

So bad

Thus, one of the six prayers the Vargas brothers prayed was answered.

And thus, on this morning long ago, the poorest village in all of Mexico suddenly became the richest.

NAME
15
rAnch
owner
brench
John

you mean you
read upside down
ARE YOU crazy
revill the next
message it's
on page
245

Mary Roach
3 Aquaview Court
Huntington L.I
11743